How You Got So SMART

by David Milgrim

G. P. Putnam's Sons • An Imprint of Penguin Group (USA) Inc.

JUST LOOK AT YOU NOW,
YOU'VE COME VERY FAR,
YOU'RE AS SHARP AS A TACK,
YOU'RE AS BRIGHT AS A STAR,

YOU'VE MADE US ALL PROUD
BY WHO YOU'VE BECOME,
AND WE'D LIKE TO REVIEW
HOW YOU DID WHAT YOU'VE DONE.

You watched the world closely.

You studied the sounds.

You had a small taste

of whatever you found.

You wandered and wondered.
You loved to explore.

For every answer you got,
you had three questions more.

You loved a good mystery.

You prodded and poked.

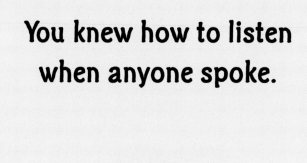

You knew how to listen
when anyone spoke.

You made a few friends.
You learned how to share.

You were never afraid to show that you care.

You gave things a try.
You were brave and courageous.

You liked to do things
that were wild and outrageous.

You loved to be challenged.
You wanted to fly.

The more that you failed,
the harder you tried.

You put things together
to see what they made.

When life gave you lemons,
you made lemonade.

You learned it's okay
if you cry when you're sad

and how to express yourself
when you are mad.

You had many teachers.
You learned from them well.

You had your own stories
you needed to tell.

You played your own music.
You sang with your heart.

And look at you now . . .
you're so brilliantly smart.

You got where you're going.
You did it your way.

Three cheers for you . . .

HIP! HIP! HOORAY!

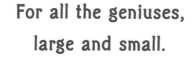

For all the geniuses,
large and small.

G. P. PUTNAM'S SONS
A division of Penguin Young Readers Group.
Published by The Penguin Group.
Penguin Group (USA) Inc., 375 Hudson Street, New York, NY 10014, U.S.A.
Penguin Group (Canada), 90 Eglinton Avenue East, Suite 700, Toronto, Ontario M4P 2Y3, Canada
(a division of Pearson Penguin Canada Inc.).
Penguin Books Ltd, 80 Strand, London WC2R 0RL, England.
Penguin Ireland, 25 St. Stephen's Green, Dublin 2, Ireland (a division of Penguin Books Ltd.).
Penguin Group (Australia), 250 Camberwell Road, Camberwell, Victoria 3124, Australia
(a division of Pearson Australia Group Pty Ltd).
Penguin Books India Pvt Ltd, 11 Community Centre, Panchsheel Park, New Delhi - 110 017, India.
Penguin Group (NZ), 67 Apollo Drive, Rosedale, North Shore 0632, New Zealand
(a division of Pearson New Zealand Ltd).
Penguin Books (South Africa) (Pty) Ltd, 24 Sturdee Avenue, Rosebank, Johannesburg 2196, South Africa.
Penguin Books Ltd, Registered Offices: 80 Strand, London WC2R 0RL, England.

Copyright © 2010 by David Milgrim.
All rights reserved. This book, or parts thereof, may not be reproduced in any form
without permission in writing from the publisher, G. P. Putnam's Sons, a division of Penguin Young Readers Group,
345 Hudson Street, New York, NY 10014. G. P. Putnam's Sons, Reg. U.S. Pat. & Tm. Off.
The scanning, uploading and distribution of this book via the Internet or via any other means without the permission
of the publisher is illegal and punishable by law. Please purchase only authorized electronic editions,
and do not participate in or encourage electronic piracy of copyrighted materials. Your support of
the author's rights is appreciated. The publisher does not have any control over and does not assume
any responsibility for author or third-party websites or their content.
Published simultaneously in Canada. Manufactured in China by South China Printing Co. Ltd.
Design by Katrina Damkoehler. Text set in Clichee Bold.
The art was done in digital ink and digital oil pastel.

Library of Congress Cataloging-in-Publication Data
Milgrim, David.
How you got so smart / David Milgrim.   p. cm.
Summary: Loved ones remind a little boy of how far he has come
and how much he has learned and accomplished along the way.
[1. Stories in rhyme. 2. Learning—Fiction. 3. Growth—Fiction. 4. Individuality—Fiction.] I. Title.
PZ8.3.M5776How 2010   [E]—dc22   2009022193

ISBN 978-0-399-25260-0
1 3 5 7 9 10 8 6 4 2